RISK YOUR LIFE ARCADE

CHOOSE YOUR OWN

NIGHTMARE...

titles in Large-Print Editions:

NIGHTMARE... #6

RISK YOUR LIFE ARCADE
BY KEN McMURTRY

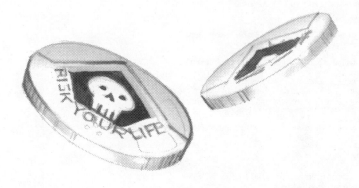

ILLUSTRATED BY BILL SCHMIDT

An R. A. Montgomery Book

Gareth Stevens Publishing
MILWAUKEE

Amer. Media
    Corp.

j

4/96

11.95

**For a free color catalog describing Gareth Stevens' list of high-quality books,
call 1-800-542-2595 (USA) or 1-800-461-9120 (Canada).
Gareth Stevens' Fax: (414) 225-0377.**

Library of Congress Cataloging-in-Publication Data

McMurtry, Ken.
     Risk Your Life Arcade / by Ken McMurtry; illustrated by
  Bill Schmidt.
        p. cm. — (Choose your own nightmare)
     Summary: The reader's decisions control the course of an adventure
  in which an evil arcade owner lures players to his home, where he
  engages them in the ultimate life-or-death game.
        ISBN 0-8368-1515-7 (lib. bdg.)
     1. Plot-your-own stories. [1. Video games—Fiction. 2. Plot-your-
  own stories.] I. Schmidt, Bill, ill. II. Title. III. Series.
  PZ7.M47879283Ri 1996
  [Fic]—dc20   95-39817

This edition first published in 1996 by
Gareth Stevens Publishing
1555 North RiverCenter Drive, Suite 201
Milwaukee, Wisconsin 53212 USA

Printed in the United States of America

1 2 3 4 5 6 7 8 9 99 98 97 96

*This book is dedicated to my son
Gabe McMurtry,
friend, advisor, and computer genius.*

WARNING!

You have probably read books where scary things happen to people. Well, in *Choose Your Own Nightmare*, you're right in the middle of the action. The scary things are happening to you!

You'll do just about anything to get your good-luck baseball cap back . . . but what does scary Mr. Sticks have in mind?

Fortunately, while you're reading along, you'll have chances to decide what to do. Whenever you make a decision, turn to the page shown. The thrills and chills that happen to you next will depend on your choices.

Make sure you choose carefully. After all, you're playing for your life.

"Yes!" you shout, pumping your fist in the air.

It is 4:00 P.M. Thursday, and you and your friends Sara and Joey are at the Risk Your Life Arcade at the Bristol Pines Mall. The place is filled with colored lights, bells, and buzzers. Kids jam in two and three deep playing the various machines, and loud music screams from the speakers scattered around the room.

You hang out here a lot. That's because this is the only arcade in town that has your favorite game—Worm Wars. "It's totally cool—kind of like the pinball machines you guys used to play when you were kids," you explained to your parents. "But much better."

Turn to page 2.

2

Worm Wars looks something like a regular pinball machine. It has a lit-up, glass-enclosed table. And there's lots of cool stuff to bounce the balls off—worm lairs, fishhooks, little metal chutes. But instead of being a one-shot-only game, Worm Wars has a real story to it. Blurgon is the king of worms. His huge, wormy body is pictured on the machine's backboard. The thing about Blurgon is that he's hungry. Real hungry. The point of the game is to try to satisfy his appetite by scoring lots of points. The more points you score, the more worms Blurgon gets to eat. And Blurgon remembers you. You type in your initials—your code name—and Blurgon says things like *"Give me more fishbait, tuna breath!"* or *"It took you fifteen minutes to fill me up last time!"* The voice is kind of scary. And it's loud—it's in digital stereo.

Go on to the next page.

It's important to fill Blurgon up, because if you make him happy, he'll give you extra balls. And sometimes if your ball slips past the flippers, Blurgon will shoot it back out to you. You get three balls per game, but if you rack up enough points, you get a speed ball—a super-fast pinball that looks like a ball of worms. It's just about the best arcade game ever invented, you think.

And right now you're playing the best you've ever played.

One reason you're doing so well is your lucky hat. It's a blue baseball cap with gold lightning bolts on either side. Just above the bill it says WORM WARS. No one else in the arcade has one like it. You wrote to the company that makes the game to tell them how much you liked it, and as a present, they sent you the hat. Now you never play a game without it. No one can beat you at Worm Wars when you're wearing your lucky cap.

"C'mon!" shouts Sara, jumping up and down. "You're doing it! You're beating your best score!"

Turn to page 4.

4

Joey slugs her in the arm. "Pipe down!" he says. "Do you want to make the Flipstar lose the game?" Flipstar is what Joey calls you when you're playing really well.

"Don't hit me!" says Sara, giving Joey a shove. The two of them begin to argue back and forth. You try not to watch. You're on your third ball—just a few points away from getting a super speed ball.

You focus on the Lair of the Worm—every time the ball goes there you get a ton of points. You're going to try to aim the ball there when it hits the flippers.

Waiting, waiting . . . *Bam!* Suddenly Joey falls against the machine.

"Hey!" you shout, accidentally jamming your finger down on the flipper. The ball hits the flipper, shoots up, and smoothly enters the Lair of the Worm.

"Good work, FSR!" Blurgon grumbles. *"A whole mouthful of worms to enjoy."* FSR is your code name. It stands for Flipstar.

Go to the next page.

You shoot a quick glance at Sara and Joey. "Would you two knock it off?" you snap. You really like your friends, but sometimes they joke around too much. "You're lucky you two losers didn't make me lose! Don't bump the machine!"

"Sorry," Joey says sheepishly.

"Yeah. Sorry," says Sara.

Joey looks at your score. "You are playing excellent!" he shouts. "The Flipstar strikes again!" He and Sara huddle around you.

Taking a deep breath, you stand poised at the flippers. "Okay. Catch and pass. Catch and pass," you chant, waiting for the ball to come down and hit the left flipper. Catching and passing is your secret weapon. Instead of hitting the ball upward, you're going to stop and catch it with one flipper, pass it to the tip of the other flipper, and shoot. It's a flawless way to score—and it's taken you months to perfect it.

"Catch and pass, catch and pass, catch and—"

Whish! Suddenly you feel something pull at your hair. Your cap! Your good-luck baseball cap has been stolen!

Turn to page 6.

6

"*What—*" you shriek, spinning around. Lefty, the weird guy who hands out tokens and fixes the arcade machines when they break down, is standing behind you. He is very short—not more than five feet tall. And he has only one arm—his right. Dangling from his right hand is your cap.

"What did you do that for?" you cry, touching your head where the cap used to be. *"Game over, Worm Head,"* gurgles Blurgon. Helplessly you watch as your last ball slips past the flippers. NEW PLAYER flashes on the blinking scoreboard.

Lefty stares at you. "You were tilting the machine," he says. "You shouldn't have been doing that."

"I was not!" you protest. "Joey bumped it by accident! That doesn't count as tilting!"

Just then Eddie Wrigley, the biggest bully in Bristol Pines, saunters over. "Hey, Lefty. Someone lose their hat?" He tucks a piece of his dark, oily hair behind his ear.

Turn to page 61.

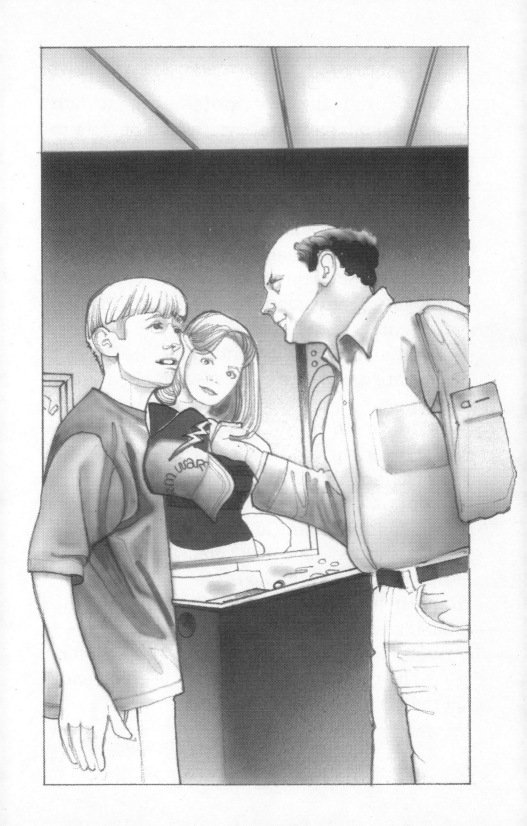

A jerk like Eddie isn't worth messing with. If you got the high score once, you'll be able to do it again.

"Go ahead. Play," you tell him. "I've got to catch up with my friends, anyway." You pick up your backpack and start to head out the arcade door. But you can't help feeling a little curious—you do want to watch Eddie play. You know he's pretty good—but he's never beaten your score.

Quietly you move behind Eddie. He doesn't even notice you—he's already wrapped up in the game.

Eddie is not very good-looking to begin with. But right now he looks worse than he ever has, you think. His face has taken on a demonic look. His beady little eyes have narrowed, and the veins are bulging on his neck. Even his greasy hair looks greasier.

To your dismay, Eddie is playing really well. You watch as he zealously flips and zings the pinballs, sending them smashing toward more points. *"Good food. Good food!"* gurgles Blurgon. The giant worm can hardly keep up with all the points Eddie is scoring.

Turn to page 38.

"You two are my very best Worm Wars players. The tournament, then, has to be the very
best as well—the ultimate Worm Wars tournament!"

"Yo, Mr. Sticks—it's me, Eddie. Remember?"
Eddie yells out worriedly. "You can't mean that
I have to play this. You and I are tight—we're
friends, right?"

"Eddie, Eddie, Eddie," says Mr. Sticks. His
voice is loud and clear on the speaker. "The
only friend you have here is yourself. Now I
suggest you get ready to play . . . for your life."

Suddenly the lights come back on. There's
no time to run. Mr. Sticks would definitely
catch you. You look at Eddie. He doesn't look
so mean right now. In fact, he looks kind of
frightened.

Turn to page 35.

10

You can't sit and watch Eddie die. "Eddie, you've got to let go of that worm. That's the poison worm—the one you're not supposed to touch!"

Eddie gives you a funny look. "You think I'm going to fall for that?" he asks. "I know Worm Wars. There's no poison worm."

You shake your head. "There is! I found it out when I scored two hundred and fifty thousand points. We must have that many now. You've got to let go! Here!" You reach out your arm to help pull him up.

"No way!" he laughs. Suddenly the worm's head begins to move. Soon its whole body is shaking.

You watch Eddie's face fall. *"Aieeee!"* he shrieks, letting go of the worm. You try to reach out to him, but it's too late. He slides down the floor of the machine, banging into various sensors and lights.

Turn to page 12.

You, Joey, and Sara hurry out of the arcade. Looking over your shoulder, you see Lefty standing in the middle of the arcade, fingering the tokens in his right hand.

"Man, that guy is strange," says Joey. The three of you walk along the sidewalk that leads from the mall to your homes. Bristol Pines is pretty small—everything is within walking distance. The sky is overcast. It looks as if a big storm is brewing.

Turn to page 64.

Bang! Eddie crashes headfirst into a flipper—and the flipper hits him. Hard. You cringe as he's sent flying past you. Your cap soars off your head. You reach out and manage to grab it as it falls. Setting it back on your head, you watch helplessly as Eddie is sucked down the Worm Tunnel.

"Good food," gurgles Blurgon. Your heart is racing as you cling to the metal chute. Is Eddie really worm food?

"We have a winner!" a voice announces. "Please let go of the chute and slide feetfirst to the bottom of the machine."

You have no choice but to comply. Nervously you let go of the chute and slither down to the bottom of the machine. The flippers open up, and you find yourself falling through the ball drop.

Turn to page 52.

A few minutes later, Mr. Sticks hurries past you, your cap tucked under his arm. Lefty is right behind him. "I'm going to put this in my house for safekeeping," you hear Mr. Sticks tell Lefty. "Then I've got to run some errands. I'll be home late tonight if you need anything." Mr. Sticks shakes Lefty's right hand and turns to glare at you. Before you can muster up the courage to say anything to him, he's gone.

"He shouldn't have taken your hat," Joey says.

"He won't have it for long," you say. "It's my hat and I'm getting it back."

"How?" asks Sara.

"I'll just wait a few minutes until I know he's had time to drop it off. Then I'll go to his house, get it, and leave before he even knows I was there. Easy," you say.

Turn to page 84.

14

Mr. Sticks drops the worm and bends down, his smelly breath hitting you smack in the face. "I'm many things to many people," he says. "The worm of Worm Wars. That's me. And this is my home. The wormhole."

"Let me go!" you shriek.

Mr. Sticks laughs. "No one's holding you. But don't bother struggling. Now that you've found this place, you'll never leave. Worm Wars sought you out. I needed a new guardian for my home. Someone who would understand the worm world as I do. And I've found that in you. And now that you're here, we'll never let you go."

Turn to page 85.

You make sure you've got a tight grip on the chute. There's no telling what would happen if you fell into the Lair of the Worm. Or worse yet, if you hit the flippers.

"Ahhhhhhh!" screams a terror-filled voice. You look frantically around the machine, trying to see who screamed. In a flash of lights, something shoots by you. It's not a pinball—it's Eddie!

Turn to page 62.

16

"Bye," you say, continuing down the street.

"Do you have a lot of homework tonight?" asks Sara.

"Nah, not really," you say truthfully.

"Well, why don't you come and stay over? You can practice on the Sega—and besides, we've got the Frankenstein." Sara grins.

Sara's house has always been fun to hang out in, but it's even better since the Frankenstein arrived. The Frankenstein is the name of the pinball machine Sara's dad has in the basement family room. When the Bristol Pines Diner closed last year, they had a big auction to get rid of all sorts of stuff. One item was the Frankenstein. Sara's dad loves pinball machines almost as much as you do. The Frankenstein was in pretty bad shape, but he got it repaired, and now it works perfectly.

"Well . . . ," you say, thinking for a minute.

Turn to page 49.

A panel in the wall slides open. Inside, on a wooden shelf, are a mask and a sack made out of black cloth. You pick them up.

"You have three seconds to put the mask on and take the bag," says the voice. "Three seconds."

You quickly put on the mask and sling the black bag over your shoulder. The panel slides shut. The lights lower, and soon you are in total darkness. You stand there nervously, wondering what will happen to you.

The wall in front of you slides open. Behind it lies what looks like a gigantic maze.

"I'm getting out of here," you say. The sound of your footsteps echoes off the high walls of the maze. You move forward cautiously, expecting some sort of surprise.

"You are the chosen one," says the voice. "And now, for the ultimate Rat Race player, here is the ultimate game. A life-size version."

"Huh?" you say. "The ultimate Rat Race player? I've never played that game in my life," you protest. "There must be some kind of mistake! I'm a Worm Wars Warrior, not a Rat Racer!"

Turn to page 82.

Your hat sits several feet in front of you. All you have to do is grab it and run. Slowly you move toward it. It seems to take you forever to get there. Now you're only a foot away. You reach out your hand to grab the hat—but then you stop.

A wave of curiosity washes over you. You know that Mr. Sticks won't be home for a while. You've secretly wondered what kind of house the weird arcade owner lives in. Now you've got the perfect chance to explore.

If you decide to explore Mr. Sticks's house, turn to page 24.

If you decide to grab your hat and leave immediately, turn to page 74.

Sara shares a room with her younger sister Abby. You sleep in the guest room, which is next door.

After a good night's sleep, you wake up to bright sunshine. A hand-lettered poster is tacked up on the bedroom door. It reads FUTURE WORM WARS CHAMP SLEPT HERE. Below the words is a drawing of your face—it looks pretty accurate. How did Sara sneak in and do that while you were sleeping? you wonder. She must have been really quiet.

Then you notice some Gummi Worms draped over the doorknob. Several more are hanging over a picture frame. There are even a few scattered on your bed.

Turn to page 78.

"Good morning, everyone!" says a loud voice. It's Mr. Lewis. He's the vice president of the Bristol Pines Bank. But instead of wearing his normal suit and tie, he's dressed in a plaid cotton shirt, fishing hat, khakis, and thigh-high yellow wading boots.

"What a great day for fishing!" he says in a singsong voice. "Abby, what's the progress?" he yells out the back door.

"Great!" yells Sara's little sister. She bursts into the room, holding a large rusted coffee can. She walks over to you.

"See?" she asks, showing you the can. It's swarming with worms. "It's a perfect day for worm hunting."

"Nice." You nod slowly.

Mr. Lewis pats you on the back. "Nothing's too good for our little Worm Wars Warrior."

You smile weakly. The Lewis family is acting pretty strange this morning—and they are one of the most normal families you know. What has gotten into them?

Turn to page 25.

"Uh . . . are you going to call the police?" you whisper. You try to avoid staring into his eyes. But it's not easy—they're only a few inches from yours.

"No," says Mr. Sticks. "No, that won't be necessary. I've been looking for someone to help me out. And I think you're just the person."

Help him out? You don't want to help him out—you want help in *getting* out! There is no way you're helping this weirdo. He probably wants to trap you in his house and hold you prisoner! He probably wants to torture you! What have you gotten yourself into?

"Now," says Mr. Sticks. He moves back a few inches, and you take a deep breath. "I'm trying to think what you'd like most. Being trapped in a room with invisible biting bugs, or fighting your way through a forest of mutants." He studies your face for a few moments.

You are frozen with fear. "In-In-Invisible biting bugs?" you croak. How can he do this to you? You wish he *would* call the police. Anything would be better than being trapped in this horrible old house with this madman.

Turn to page 56.

"It's almost closing time, anyway," Joey says persistently.

"My mom will be mad at me if I hang out too late," Sara says. "Besides, we're out of tokens. Joey's right. We should head for home."

"I'm not leaving," you say. *Flip! Flip!* The ball shoots up into the Worm Tunnel. "Cool! Twenty-five thousand extra points!" you yell.

Your friends shake their heads. "Well, we're leaving," Sara says. "See you tomorrow."

You stay glued to the machine, losing all track of time. Your score is growing and growing. Not only have you beat your highest score, it looks as if you're going to beat the all-time greatest Worm Wars score, too! The initials NLA have been at the top of the screen for months. You don't know who NLA is—the only person you've ever seen play Worm Wars as well as you is Eddie Wrigley, and his code initials are EWW.

Carefully you try to nudge the ball around the machine. *"Thanks for all the food!"* bellows Blurgon in digital sound.

"You're welcome!" you say happily. "Gettin' ready to feed you more!"

Turn to page 28.

"Negative. I want to get home before the storm hits," you say, pointing up at the sky.

"All right," Sara says. You've arrived at your turnoff. "Call me later."

"Yep," you say, waving good-bye. As you walk, a slight drizzle rains down on you. You wish you had listened to your mom—she wanted you to wear your rain slicker today. You hate getting wet. Luckily you have your umbrella—it's nice and big.

Slap, slap, slap. Your sneakers splash through the puddles. For such a little drizzle, the puddles certainly are forming quickly, you think. Maybe it rained over this part of town already.

Soon the rain begins to come down harder. It's raining at a slant, and the water is spraying you in the face every few seconds. It has also grown very, very foggy. It's almost impossible to see more than a few feet in front of you.

"Darn this rain!" you say, picking up speed. You can't wait to get home to a cup of your mom's hot chocolate.

Without warning, a gust of wind blows your umbrella inside out.

Turn to page 26.

24

Now that you're here, you suppose it wouldn't hurt to have a look around. The house is much bigger than it looks from the outside. To your right is a hallway. Near the end of it, stairs curve up to the second floor. The living room has a couch and a few shabby chairs. In the back is a doorway.

You walk across the living room and through the door. It looks like some sort of study. A large mahogany desk sits in the corner. A tiny desk lamp on it throws a pale white cast across the room. Bookshelves containing old, dusty books line the walls. You notice that a lot of them have to do with games—their rules, inventions, that sort of thing. And you notice another door.

Walking through it, you find yourself in some kind of game room. Several large ceiling lights shine brightly. Along one wall are soft, comfortable-looking chairs, much nicer than the ones in the living room. Opposite them is a row of arcade games—about five or six. They are all lit up, waiting.

Turn to page 76.

"Here—have a bowl of cereal," says Mrs. Lewis, putting a bowl of cornflakes in front of you. "Oops! Forgot the topping."

Mrs. Lewis is great. She always remembers to put banana slices on top—just the way you like it.

To your horror, she reaches into Abby's can and pulls out a handful of worms.

"Here," she says, dropping them in your bowl. "This ought to taste really good!"

You push your chair back from the table. What is going on here? The Lewises were fine last night—but now they're worm-obsessed!

Turn to page 72.

"Hey!" you shout, trying to pull the nylon down over the spokes. The wind howls around you as you struggle with the umbrella. But it's no use. The umbrella is worthless.

"Great. Just great," you mutter. You realize the fog has gotten even thicker. Even though you've walked this way millions of times, it's now impossible to see. You can't tell which way to go.

Trying to regain your sense of direction, you decide that your house must be to your left. Clutching your broken umbrella, you begin to run, splashing through puddle after puddle.

"Almost there! Almost there! Almost— *Ahhh!*" Your foot slips, and you fall into the biggest puddle you've ever seen.

"Gross!" you say, pulling a fat purple worm off your arm. Before you can get up, someone yanks the back of your shirt, and you fall back into the puddle.

"Welcome home," says a low whisper. You try to turn around, but something is holding you down.

Turn to page 55.

Just as you're ready to pull back the plunger on your next ball, somebody shoves you. Hard. You lose your balance and fall against the Monster Squasher machine to your left.

"You've hogged the machine long enough, Chickenhead!" It's Eddie Wrigley. He puts his hand on the plunger, as if he's about to pull it.

"No!" you shout, scrambling up. "You'll screw up my score!"

"What are you going to do about it?" Eddie asks. "No one's here to help you now."

You look around. He's right. Somehow the arcade has emptied out without your even knowing it. You guess you were too wrapped up in the Worm Wars game to even notice.

One thing's for sure—you're tired of Eddie bullying you around. And you don't like getting shoved. More than anything you'd like to shove *him* and regain your position at the controls. But he is a big bully—he'll probably try to start a real fight.

If you decide he's too mean to mess with, turn to page 8.

If you push Eddie out of the way, turn to page 51.

It doesn't seem as if you're ever going to find your way out of the maze. You have found quite a bit of cheese, though. In fact, your pack is bulging with it.

"If only I had some crackers," you say to yourself, trying to make a joke. But you don't feel much like laughing right now. Stopping to take a breath, you sit on the ground. You feel as if you've been collecting cheese for hours, yet you don't feel any closer to getting out.

In the distance you hear what sounds like someone running. You listen more closely. No, it doesn't sound like *one* person running—it sounds like a hundred!

You know you should probably run, but you feel frozen with fear. Gripping the cheese bag as tightly as you can, you force yourself to stand up. Then you dash to your left, away from the sound.

Must be Mr. Sticks and Lefty. Got to get out of here. Got to make it out alive!

You race down the maze—and then come screeching to a halt.

Turn to page 70.

30

But you can't quit yet—you've earned not one but three super speed balls. Confidently you pull the plunger, your fingers poised on the controls. Your left arm is starting to ache. You try to ignore it, but you can't. It really hurts.

"Too much playing, I guess," you say reluctantly. "Maybe I should quit." You try to pull your arm up to rub it, but you can't. It's as if your fingers are glued to the flipper.

Turn to page 60.

"So, you've lost your hat," Eddie sneers.

"I didn't lose it," you answer. "Lefty stole it. He just wants you to have a chance in the Worm Wars tournament."

Eddie frowns. "Hey, I can beat you with or without your lucky hat."

"I don't think you can," Sara says. "You're always doing odd jobs here for Lefty and Mr. Sticks, trying to be their friend. I bet you asked Lefty to take the hat, just so you could win!"

Eddie glares at Sara. "I can beat Chickenhead here, hat or no hat."

"Sara's right," Joey says, moving closer to Eddie.

"Who are you?" Eddie says, pointing a finger at Joey. "Chickenhead's shadow?"

"Stop calling me Chickenhead," you say.

"Or what?"

"Or I'll—" You break off as Eddie turns away. Mr. Sticks is signaling to him from the back of the arcade.

"I have to go now. But don't think I've forgotten about you," Eddie says menacingly. "Chickenhead." He turns and pushes his way through the crowd of kids.

Turn to page 39.

You can't believe it. Mr. Sticks has actually turned his house into a living arcade game.

Suddenly the pole you're holding on to lights up. Startled, you let go and tumble forward, falling headfirst down the slippery machine floor. Below you flashes a dark brown hole.

"Oh no!" you cry. The Lair of the Worm is waiting to devour you! You've got to stop your fall. Quickly you reach out and grab hold of the metal chute that cuts across the machine. The chute is always a good place to send a ball—it really makes them fly.

Heaving a sigh of relief, you take a look around you.

It's incredible. Every detail of Worm Wars, down to the exact colors, is here. You wonder how Mr. Sticks did it. And why.

Bing bing! Diloop! Feeeeeloop! The sound is so loud you have to cover your ears. You know what that sound means—a ball has just been released into the game.

Turn to page 15.

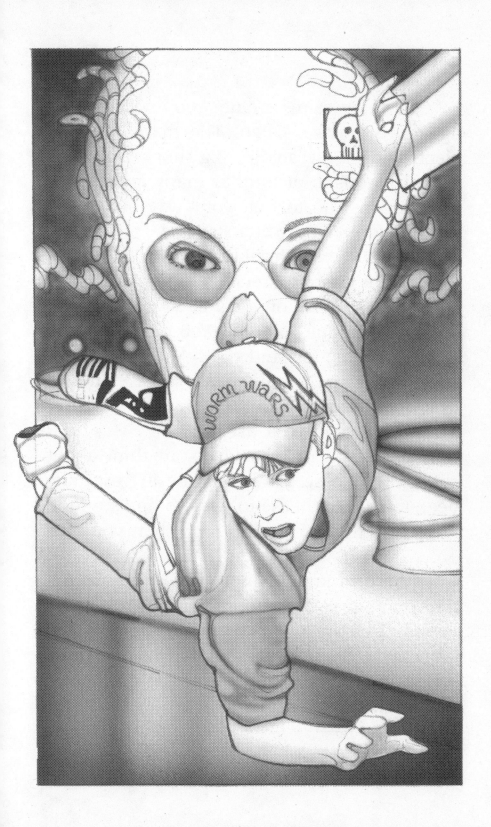

"Can you give me a clue?" you yell, leaning against the maze. Ouch! The maze must be electrified—it gives you a big shock.

"Your job is to pick up as many accessories as you can, and to find your way out of the maze before you are attacked."

"Attacked?" you shriek.

"You are wasting precious time. Remember to keep your mask on. Begin!" says the voice.

There's no time to argue. You race down the maze, glancing left and right. You spot something yellow in the corner. What is it? You race over and discover that it is a hunk of cheese—about the size of your fist.

You remember Joey saying something about collecting cheese. That must be it! You must need to collect cheese to win! You pick up the hunk and throw it in the bag. Then you race on.

It's hard to know which way to go—sometimes you go left, sometimes right. You guess you must be the only player in the maze. A few times you hear what sounds like someone scratching on the other side of the maze wall, but you don't run into anyone.

Turn to page 29.

"Listen, I just came for my hat," you say. "I haven't paid the fee for entering the tournament, so I guess I should be going." You try to sound confident.

Mr. Sticks's laugh crackles through the speaker. "I would have been very disappointed if you hadn't come. And for a champion player like you, the tournament fee is waived."

"What kind of sick joke is this?" Eddie yells.

"It's no joke. It's just what I said," says Mr. Sticks. "A game. If you lose, you die. It's simple. Now, I want both of you to shake hands and walk through the Start door."

To your right is a bright red door that you somehow missed seeing earlier. A sign on it says Start in thick white letters.

You really don't want to do this, but you don't have a choice. Warily you stick out your hand to Eddie. "Well, good luck," you say.

"Yeah. Good luck," Eddie says, sticking out his greasy hand. He looks very scared. Just as you're about to shake his hand, he whips it up and snatches the cap off your head. "Get ready to lose!" he yells, racing to the door.

Turn to page 36.

You try to catch him, but he's too fast. You run through the Start door. A long, narrow hallway lies ahead of you. Eddie and your cap are nowhere in sight. You wonder where he is.

A draft of wind blows through the hallway. *Pow!* Something really hard punches you in the back, shooting you down the hall.

"Whoaaaa!" you scream in terror. You curl your body up in a ball to avoid hitting the wall. You can't believe how fast you're moving.

Then, just as fast, you find yourself in a gigantic arcade. Everywhere you look, lights are flashing, and sirens are buzzing. It's so loud it makes you want to cover your ears. You can't quite put your finger on it, but something about the arcade looks really familiar.

Turn to page 47.

You had to write to the head of the Life-or-Death arcade manufacturing company to get that hat, and you are not about to give it up so easily.

"I'm going to get my cap back," you say. "Are you guys coming or not?"

Sara and Joey look at each other nervously.

"Well . . . I really shouldn't. I'm going to have to get going soon anyway," Sara tells you. "My parents will be sending out the National Guard if I'm not home soon."

"And I've been waiting to play Rat Race all afternoon," says Joey, pointing to his favorite game. A kid is just getting up from the seat. "I'm not going to leave now just to get your dumb old cap."

"My cap is not dumb," you say angrily. "What's dumb is that game."

"Whatever. Good luck," says Joey, running over to Rat Race.

Sara gives you a worried look. "Are you sure you want to go alone?"

"Yes, I'm sure. I'll just get my cap and get out of there before Sticks ever returns."

"Okay," says Sara. "But be careful."

Turn to page 69.

"I did it!" Eddie screams as the flashing point scorer goes over the top score, beating NLA. "I did it!" Blurgon's whole body has taken on an eerie glow, and sounds you've never heard before—almost like sirens—peal out from the machine.

You feel sick to your stomach because Eddie has played so well. Now you'll never hear the end of it.

"Dumb luck," you say, shaking your head. You look up at the score box one more time.

To your surprise, the score has disappeared. Small boxes have opened up somehow on the backboard. Hundreds of tiny grayish-blue worms are spilling out of the machine—and all over Eddie!

Turn to page 66.

There is a brief moment of silence. "Thanks for sticking up for me," you say finally.

"That Eddie is such a loser," Sara says.

"Yeah," says Joey. "What a moron."

You shrug. "Who cares about Eddie? I just want my hat!" You kick the bottom of the game next to Worm Wars. "Can you believe that Lefty? He's the moron! How can he do this to me? There's only two days left!"

This coming Saturday is the day you've been preparing for for weeks—it's the National Worm Wars Tournament. You and forty-nine other players from around the country have been selected to compete. Lucky for you, the tournament is being held right here in Bristol Pines. "I'm going to get that hat back—even if I have to go to Mr. Sticks myself!" you say.

"No hat is worth risking a run-in with Mr. Sticks," Joey says.

Turn to page 68.

40

The Risk Your Life Arcade is next to the Twin Cinemas, just off the mall's food court. The arcade used to be called the Playtime Arcade. That was until Mr. Sticks moved to town and bought it and changed the name. It sounded weird to you at first. But you're used to it now. Even though you don't like Mr. Sticks, you love his games. He's replaced a lot of the old, outdated stuff with cool, new, exciting games—games that no other arcade in town has.

Turn to page 13.

Lefty shakes his head. "No can do. Mr. Sticks wants to examine it. When he's through, you'll get it back." He reaches into his right pocket. "Let me give you a few tokens to make it up to you. On the house." Lefty winks at Sara and Joey. "And I'm sure you two won't tell if I reset the game to where the Flipstar was before he lost his cap."

Sara's and Joey's mouths fall open in shock.

You don't know what to say. Why is Lefty being so nice to you? Can you trust him? Normally you would say no. But you have run out of tokens . . . and you really need to practice.

If you accept Lefty's offer of tokens,
turn to page 42.

If you refuse the tokens,
turn to page 63.

42

"Uh . . . thanks, I guess," you say, reaching for the tokens. You're careful not to let Lefty's hand touch yours. The tokens fall into your palm. They feel sleek and cool.

"Enjoy," says Lefty. He smiles and merges into the crowd of kids surging through the arcade.

"Hey, look at these," you say, examining the tokens. The regular Risk Your Life tokens are gold. The ones Lefty has given you are shiny purple. They have a little worm imprinted on them.

"Cool!" says Joey. "Personalized Worm Wars tokens!"

"I wonder if they have them for Queen Beheader," Sara says. Queen Beheader is her favorite game.

"Why don't you go ask Lefty?" you ask.

"I don't think so," says Sara, giving a shiver. "He's too weird. I've got one token left I can use." She heads across the room toward Queen Beheader.

Turn to page 54.

A worm like Eddie deserves to be attacked by a worm, you think. Why should you help him out?

Bing bing! Diloop! Feeeeeloop! Peerooooop! Another ball has been released. You can hear it rattling through the machine—it sounds really fast. With a start, you realize it's the super speed ball.

The ball is getting closer and closer. It sounds as if it's right above you. It is! Like lightning, the ball comes hurtling over the chute—and right over your hands.

"Ahhh!" you scream, letting go of the chute. The pain is intense. As you fall, you catch a brief glimpse of Eddie holding on to the worm. Nothing's happened to him yet.

"So long, loser!" he yells.

You plummet toward the waiting flippers.

The End

44

He laughs. "Glad you stopped when you did, huh?" he asks.

You try to answer him, but nothing comes out. Your mouth moving wordlessly, you push past him and break into a run. Within seconds you're standing in the food court of the Bristol Pines Mall.

Sara and Joey will never believe it, but it's true—you will never, ever play Worm Wars again.

The End

Turning to face the porch, you cross to a narrow window. It's open, and a slight breeze is blowing the lace curtains outward. You stoop down and peek in. For an instant you think you see a flicker. But you decide it's just your head playing tricks on you. There, on a small wooden end table, sits your cap. Lightning bolts glimmer in the near-darkness.

"Okay," you say, trying to reassure yourself. "I'll just crawl through the window, go over to the table, grab my cap, and leave." Making sure no one sees you, you crawl through the open window and step into what seems to be the living room. Even though you're sure you're alone, you try not to make any noise. Looking around, you see that the house has very high ceilings. It smells musty inside, like something very old and damp. Maybe that's why Sticks left the window open—to air it out.

Turn to page 18.

46

You stifle the impulse to scream. No sense in drawing attention to yourself. But you can't control the wild beating of your heart. It sounds so loud you can't believe no one else hears it. Suddenly you think you hear a noise from the living room. Has Mr. Sticks returned already? you wonder, your stomach tying itself into knots. And if he has, does he know you're here? It's time for you to get out . . . fast!

If you want to go back the way you came in,
turn to page 57.

If you decide to look for another exit,
turn to page 65.

To your surprise, you discover that the floor of the arcade is tilted. Now that the force of whatever it was that hit you has lessened, you grab on to a large pole to steady yourself—and to keep from slipping down the arcade floor.

To your surprise, you see your cap! It's dangling from a nearby silver pole. Quickly you grab the cap and stick it firmly on your head.

"Human worm. Fifty thousand points," booms a voice. You realize the voice belongs to Blurgon! Slowly it hits you.

You aren't in an arcade. You're in a life-size version of Worm Wars.

Turn to page 32.

"I wanted to make sure you didn't pull any funny stuff about getting the cap back," Eddie mutters. "So when you left the arcade, I followed you here. And then I got kind of curious. I snooped around and found a room full of games. It's unreal."

"So did I!" you say.

"Well, there must be more than one game room then, because I never saw you," Eddie says. "Thank goodness."

"So how'd you know where I was?" you ask.

"Easy," Eddie says. Even though you can't see him, you can tell he's smirking. "I heard the goofy little noise the Doom 800 makes every time you cut someone off. I knew the only Chickenhead who'd ever play that lame game was you."

"You can make fun of me all you want," you say. "But I just want to get out of here."

"Yeah, me too," says Eddie. For once the two of you agree on something. You are heading for the door of the game room together when the voice of Mr. Sticks thunders across the room.

Turn to page 59.

"Oh, come on," Sara says. "It'll be fun."

You would like to practice your game. But Lefty has made you feel kind of uneasy. Maybe you should go home. You know your mom is fixing your favorite food—spaghetti—for dinner.

*If you decide you'd better go home,
turn to page 23.*

*If you decide to go to Sara's house and practice,
turn to page 50.*

50

"Okay," you tell Sara. "I'll come."

"All right!" she says. "Race you!"

You're only a few blocks away from her house. In a flash you and Sara speed down the sidewalk. You beat her—but only by a few seconds.

"Hi, Mom," pants Sara, barreling through the front door.

"Hi there," says Mrs. Lewis. "A little late, aren't you?"

You and Sara look at each other. "Yes," says Sara. "But we were just getting ready for the big Worm Wars tournament." She points to you. "We have the future champion here in our midst!"

After calling your parents to make sure it's okay, you eat dinner with Sara's family. Her mom's chicken casserole is not as good as spaghetti, but it's not that bad. After you help with the dishes, you and Sara head down to the family room.

Turn to page 77.

Before he can pull the plunger, you shove Eddie out of the way. "No one is going to push me around!" you yell. "Now back off!"

To your surprise, Eddie listens to you. A funny look spreads across his face, but it's gone within a second. He moves behind you to watch.

Quickly you pull and release the plunger. "Yes!" you shout. "I'm going to knock you off the top, NLA!" *Flip! Flip!* Your fingers tap lightly on the flippers. "Come on, come on," you say, coaxing the ball through the Worm Wars maze. The machine is lighting up like crazy—the Lair of the Worm, the Worm Tunnel, all your favorite parts.

Then you've done it! You've beaten NLA! *"The number-one scorer is now FSR,"* intones Blurgon. The exhilaration you feel is incredible. You wish your friends were here to see this.

"Total Worm Wars domination!" you shout, slapping the sides of the game with your hands.

Turn to page 30.

The ball drop opens directly above Mr. Sticks's living room. With a hard thud, you land on the floor.

You're just about to run out the front door when Mr. Sticks walks into the room. "Please turn in your cap," he says. You don't argue—you give it to him. From his pocket he pulls out a bright green cap. WORM WARS CHAMPION, it says in bright pink, yellow, and blue embroidery. The letters are shaped like worms.

"You earned it," says Mr. Sticks, handing it to you.

"But . . . but . . . what about Eddie?" you ask.

"He's making Blurgon very happy right now," Mr. Sticks tells you. "Very, very happy."

The End

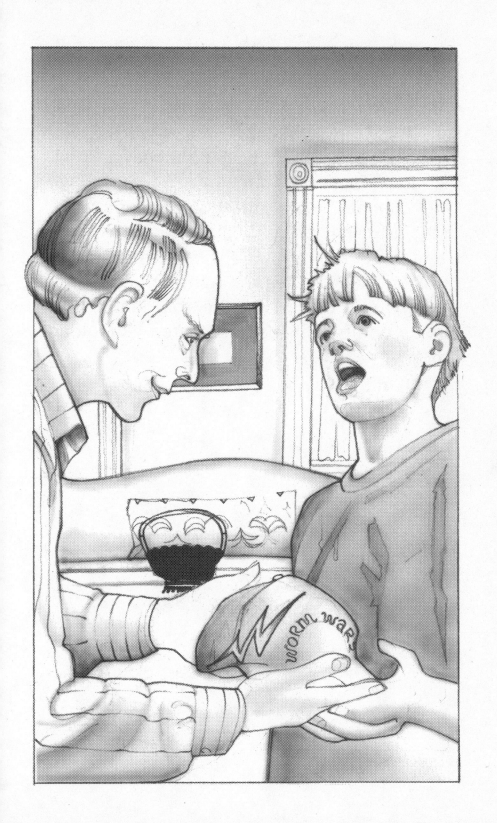

54

You drop one of the tokens into the coin slot. The game lights up. "Well, it works," you say. Carefully you pull back on the lever, sending your first ball careening forward. *Bing bing! Diloop!* The ball smashes from one target to the next. The points begin to rack up on the flashing scoreboard. *Flip! Flip!* Expertly you press on the left, then the right flipper.

Your heart beats faster as you continue to pile up points. This ball has lasted you a long time!

"You're playing fantastic!" shouts Joey.

Turn to page 83.

"Who are you?" you ask, frightened.

A laugh rings out. "I am the worm." You struggle to turn around and look up into the yellowed, wrinkled face of Mr. Sticks.

Using all your energy, you try to fight your way out of the puddle, but all you manage to do is slip and slide. The puddle is really oily.

"Mr. Sticks!" you gasp. He picks up an earthworm and begins twirling it between his fingers. "Why do you call yourself the worm?" you scream.

Turn to page 14.

"When would you like to start? Say next week?" he asks you. "After the Worm Wars tournament? You'll need to get your parents' permission, of course."

"What?" you say. "What do you mean, my parents' permission?" You are very confused. "You mean you're not going to torture me to-day?"

Turn to page 80.

Sticking with what you know, you decide to go back the way you came.

You're groping your way through the darkened game room when you bump into someone. You break out into a sweat. "Who's there?" you finally ask.

"Shhh!" says the person. "It's me. Eddie."

"Eddie Wrigley?" you squeak.

"No, Eddie Munster. Of *course* Eddie Wrigley! Now shut up!" he says, hitting you in the face with something. You cringe, but the object is soft and smells like shampoo. Your cap!

"What are you doing here?" you whisper, grabbing the cap from him. You can't believe you're stuck in an old spooky house with the biggest bully in Bristol Pines!

Turn to page 48.

"I guess I'll stay and play," you say, sighing. You put your last token into the machine. But your heart really isn't in it. The whole scene with Lefty and Eddie has left you feeling uneasy about the tournament. And you feel practically naked without your hat.

The result is you lose in a matter of minutes. *"You're a loser, FSR!"* gurgles Blurgon. His huge worm body begins to glow a deep green. You've never seen him turn that color—usually he turns red or orange.

"Wow. Even Blurgon is down on you," says Joey.

"Thanks," you say. "That makes me feel much better."

"Don't let it get to you," says Sara.

"Yeah, don't let it get to you," says a nasal voice. It's Lefty! "Sorry about the cap," he says, smiling. "Just doin' my job."

"Well, can you get it back for me, please?" you ask, surprised at Lefty's change of attitude.

Turn to page 41.

"Welcome!" he says. You realize he isn't actually in the room—his voice is coming through some kind of speaker, like the ones at the arcade. "Welcome to my house."

His voice sends shivers up and down your spine. "But it's not a home," he adds. "You thought the Worm Wars tournament was in the arcade!" He gives a sinister laugh. "But you both thought wrong. The real tournament is right here, right now!"

With a sickening feeling in your stomach, you realize Mr. Sticks has lured you to his house with your cap. If only you hadn't come to get it! Why didn't you listen to Sara and Joey?

Turn to page 9.

"Hey! What's going on?" you say.

From out of nowhere Lefty appears. He hurries over to you.

"My hand! I can't move it!" you tell him.

Lefty smiles. "Don't worry. The same thing happened to me when *I* was the all-time scorer." Your eyes widen.

"*You're* NLA? But I thought your last name was Rogers," you say.

"I use a code name just like you. NLA—No Left Arm. Get it? Anyway, about your arm. Don't worry. It's easy to fix." Lefty gives a long, hard look at your left arm. Then he takes his right arm and rubs the stump where his left arm used to be.

"Now there'll be two of us," he says. Eddie laughs.

The End

Lefty leans on the machine with his right hand and eyes you. "I knew you couldn't be that good a Worm Wars player. Eddie here told me and Mr. Sticks to keep an eye on you. He's right. You are a cheater. And now we've got you." He runs his tongue across his chapped lips.

"Yeah, you little worm," Eddie says. Eddie is about six inches taller than you, and about fifteen pounds heavier. He's always been a bully. In school you try to avoid him.

You don't even glance at Eddie. "Look," you tell Lefty, "I am not a cheater. I know techniques. I know what to go for," you add hotly. "And I'm going to prove it when I win the Worm Wars tournament." You take a deep breath. "So give me my hat. Now!"

Lefty laughs. "A real champion shouldn't need a lucky hat," he says, fingering the cap's brim. "I'll give you your hat on Saturday. After the tournament." Before you can protest, he hurries off to the rear of the arcade.

Turn to page 31.

"Helllllllp!" he screams, banging into a neon yellow sensor on the side of the machine. *"One hundred thousand points!"* gurgles Blurgon. The sensor glows and sends off a shock that propels Eddie to the other side of the machine. You watch as he slides down toward the bottom. Eddie manages to grab on to a big orange worm that's stuck to the ground. He's only inches from the right flipper.

"Okay, now what do we do?" whispers Eddie, looking at you. He's holding on to the worm for dear life. Lights and buzzers flash and sound around him.

You stare at him. You realize Eddie isn't as great a player as you. If he were, he would know that touching that worm is forbidden! It's one of Blurgon's rules.

You're not sure what to do. Should you tell Eddie to let go—and try to help him up to you? Or should you be quiet? After all, Mr. Sticks did say this game was life-or-death. And you want the life part. But how long can you hang from the chute?

If you decide to warn Eddie, turn to page 10.

If you don't say anything, turn to page 43.

"Thanks, but no thanks," you say, looking at the tokens. Even though it sounds appealing, a little voice in your head is telling you not to accept Lefty's offer. "I think I've had enough for today. C'mon," you say to Joey and Sara. "Let's go."

The three of you start to walk out of the arcade, but Lefty blocks your way.

"You can't just walk away like that," he says. "It's not that easy."

"Huh?" you say, trying to sidestep him. Instead, he moves so that you're forced to turn around and face the Worm Wars game.

Lefty points to your high score. "It's too late," he whispers.

"Yeah, big deal. I can get another high score anytime I want," you say, pushing past him. Lefty is really giving you the creeps today, and for once all you want to do is leave this place.

Turn to page 11.

"I'll say," Sara agrees. "With a guy like him in the arcade, kids are going to stop hanging out there."

"I don't know about that," you say. "The games there are way cooler than at any other arcade."

Sara kicks a branch lying across the sidewalk. "I guess," she says. "But I think I'm going to stop going there for a while. My parents keep bugging me that I never play the Sega Genesis they got me for Christmas. And I need to keep up with my homework."

You nod. With all the tournament hoopla going on, you've kind of ignored your own homework.

Soon you come to Maple Grove Road, Joey's turnoff.

"Bye, guys," he says, giving both you and Sara high fives. "No prison tomorrow!" There is an in-service day tomorrow, so school is canceled. Joey hates school.

Turn to page 16.

There's probably a shortcut out, you think. Hurriedly you exit by the rear door of the game room and find yourself in another game room. More games line the wall. Some you're familiar with, some you're not. But there's no time to play them now.

You race through the game room . . . but it only leads to another. In a panic, you run to the next room, and the next, but all you find are games.

"There must be some way to get out of this place!" you cry. You hurry through the next doorway and find yourself in a room about the size of a large closet. In the center of the room are a desk and chair. On top of the desk is a computer. *Type in your name* flashes on the screen.

You hesitate for a moment, then type in your name.

"Welcome to the Risk Your Life Home Arcade," says a computerized voice. "You will be playing at the ultimate risk level. At this level the only prize offered is your life. Good luck."

Turn to page 17.

"Ohhhh!" you gasp, stumbling backward. The worms are really long—about ten inches each—and there are thousands of them. In seconds they've wrapped around Eddie's arms, pulling him tighter and tighter against the machine.

"Nooo!" screeches Eddie. The slimy worms are now crawling on his chest, around his waist—they've even wrapped around his ears. It's totally disgusting.

Half fascinated, half repelled, you stare in shock as the giant worm image of Blurgon disappears from the backboard of Worm Wars. Another image, faint at first, begins to appear. It's Eddie's face, screaming in terror. In his hair is an entire nest of writhing, glowing worms. His skin looks almost transparent—you can see his bony skull underneath!

"Got to get out of here. Got to—" you gasp, spinning around. *Boom!* You run smack into Lefty.

Turn to page 44.

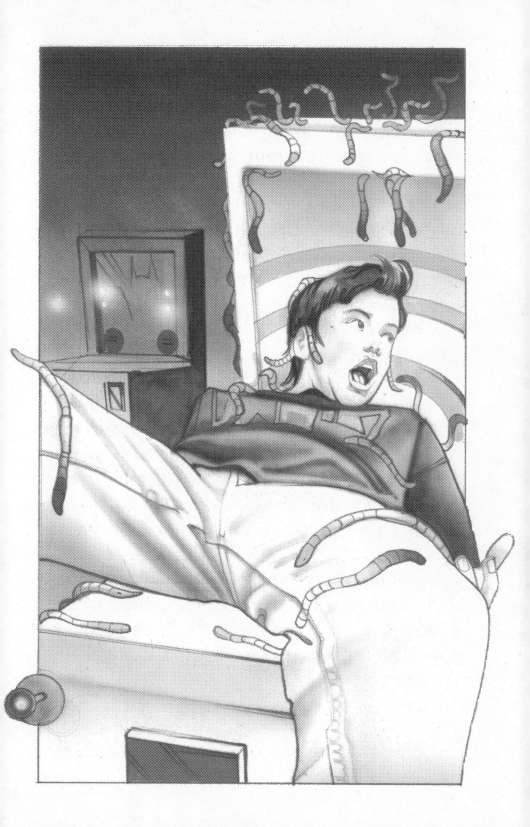

"It's the Flipstar's good-luck cap," Sara reminds him. "A champion needs all the luck they can get. The tournament starts in two days."

You and your friends look toward the back of the arcade. At first all you see are kids in jeans and T-shirts milling around. Then you see Lefty talking with Mr. Sticks. The two men look over at you.

Mr. Sticks is Risk Your Life's creepy owner. He is the thinnest, ugliest man you have ever seen. His face is like a thin wedge of wrinkled lemon pie. His skin is yellowed with age. A circle of black hair, stiff as a brush, shoots straight up from his head like a dark halo. It frames his bald spot at the top. But most unusual of all are his ears—they're long and pointed on top. They make him look like a goat.

Mr. Sticks wears a lot of weird jewelry. Rings with strange symbols—triangles, circles, lazy eights—adorn every finger of each liver-spotted hand. You think he looks like a skeleton draped with skin.

Turn to page 40.

You nod. After waiting ten minutes to make sure Mr. Sticks has had time to go home, you leave the arcade and head for his house. It's dark out now, and you're glad the house is not far from the arcade. When you get there, you notice it is the only house on the Village Green that is totally dark. A full moon hangs in the night sky, lighting it up. The house is one of the oldest in Bristol Pines. And, you think, one of the spookiest.

Good. The fact that there are no lights on must mean Mr. Sticks isn't home.

You feel the rotting wood of the first step give a little as you tiptoe up the stairs to the front porch. This place could use some major renovations, you think. A noise startles you, and you turn around. But nothing is there—all you see are the other large homes that line the Village Green. In the distance you can make out the roof of the mall.

Turn to page 45.

70

The sound of footsteps is much closer. In fact, the footsteps are on both sides of you now.

Now you remember how you get killed.

Rats. Hundreds of them. Fat, furry, dirty rats surround you. Their beady red eyes stare at one thing. Your cheese bag.

You're more than willing to feed them.

Will cheese be enough?

The End

"Look, I don't know what's gotten into you all, but you are worming me out!" you yell. "The joke's over."

"Joke?" Sara says.

"What joke?" asks Mr. Lewis.

"Is there something wrong with my worms?" asks Abby.

Mrs. Lewis holds up the bowl of cereal. "I'm going to call your mother if you don't finish this," she warns.

The four of them begin walking toward you. "Worm Wars! Worm Wars! Worm Wars!" they chant. "Eat! Eat! Eat!"

You take the bowl. The worms are squirming in the milk. The thought of putting even one worm into your mouth makes you sick to your stomach, but . . .

"It's the breakfast of the brave," says Sara. She plucks one of the worms out of the cereal and pops it into her mouth. "Yummy! Now it's *your* turn."

You can't believe what's happening.

Turn to page 79.

You decide the best thing to do is to get your hat and run. Why take chances? You wonder what could happen to you for entering Mr. Sticks's house without permission. Well, you tell yourself, at least you didn't break in. The window was open, after all. And it is your hat. It's not as if you're stealing or anything.

Leaning forward, you grab the hat. Ahhh, you think, putting it back on your head. It feels great.

And then something grabs you.

"I thought I would find you here," says a nasal, whiny voice.

It's Mr. Sticks! You turn around, feeling your stomach fall to your knees.

"Breaking into my house, destroying property—that's all very, very serious," he tells you.

"I didn't break in," you say. "And I didn't touch anything! The window was open. I . . . I just wanted to get my hat back. That's all," you tell him nervously.

He puts his face very close to yours—his nose almost touches your own. The creepy arcade owner looks even uglier up close. He doesn't say a word. He just looks at you.

Turn to page 21.

"Wow!" you say, walking over. "Here's Apple Pie Man. And the Doom 800! My favorite games!" Well, former favorites, you think, correcting yourself. Back in the old days of the Playtime Arcade, you loved playing Apple Pie Man and especially the Doom 800—where you play a character in a death-defying car chase. But Mr. Sticks got rid of those games when he opened Risk Your Life.

Or so you thought.

Turn to page 81.

You play a few games of pinball—the Frankenstein always makes you feel happy. "I feel really lucky," you say, pulling back the plunger for the third time. "I just hope I can pull it off on Saturday."

"Well, you're the best Worm Wars player in Bristol Pines," Sara reminds you. "Everyone is rooting for you."

"Everyone but Mr. Sticks and Lefty," you say glumly. "I wish they'd give me my hat back."

Sara flops down on the couch. "So what? You'll get a new hat after you win the contest. It'll say WORM WARS CHAMPION. That's even better than the hat they took."

"You're right," you say. "But I still don't like it."

"Stop thinking about them!" Sara says. "You've got to start thinking positively about the tournament. Worm Wars should be your life!"

You and Sara play for a little longer and then do some homework. Before you know it, it's time for bed.

Turn to page 19.

"I guess Sara wants me to get in the spirit," you say to yourself. You pop one of the worms into your mouth. It's a lime one. Then you get dressed and head downstairs for breakfast.

"Hi, Mrs. Lewis," you say, sliding into a chair. "Hey, Sara—you really went to town last night in my room."

Sara is pouring herself a glass of orange juice. She turns around. Hanging from her ears are long Gummi Worm earrings. "What are you talking about?" she asks, her face blank. "I was never in your room last night."

"Sure, you know," you say, laughing. "The Gummi Worms, the poster."

"Gummi Worms? Poster?" Sara repeats. She doesn't laugh. "Beats me. Maybe you dreamed it."

"No . . . I—" Your words are interrupted by heavy footsteps.

Turn to page 20.

Gulping, you take a spoonful of cereal and bring it to your lips. Two big, fat worms rear their heads. You gulp again and close your eyes.

Before you chicken out, you put the high-protein spoonful in your mouth. You chew. Your taste buds tingle. Forget bananas—your cereal has never tasted so good. And you know why: It's the worms!

Hungrily you finish the entire bowl. Then you look up. Sara, Abby, and Mr. and Mrs. Lewis are staring at you with their mouths wide open.

"I—I didn't mean for you to really eat that," says Sara. "I didn't eat a real worm. I planted one of these in your bowl." She pulls off one of her Gummi Worm earrings.

"We just wanted to help you get in the worm spirit," says Mrs. Lewis. "I'm really sorry. It was a bad joke."

You point to your cereal bowl and smile. "I'm in the spirit all right—in the spirit for a second bowl, with extra worms, please."

The End

Now Mr. Sticks is the one who looks confused. "Torture you? No, no, no! Ever since I moved to Bristol Pines, I've been looking for the right kid to test out my games. In addition to owning the arcade, I work on game development for the Life-or-Death game company. You know, the company that makes Worm Wars. And I need someone to play some of the games I've come up with. To get all the kinks out of them. Someone who likes to take risks. And by coming here to get your hat, you've proved that you're that kind of person." He smiles at you. "Are you interested?"

The offer comes as a complete surprise. "I'll think it over," you say.

"Free Worm Wars tokens for life," Mr. Sticks says.

"Well, then—you've got a deal!" you say. "But my parents have to okay it first," you add.

"Great," says Mr. Sticks. "Now I've finally found my two testers."

"Two testers?" you ask. "Who else is doing it?"

"That nice boy from the arcade. Eddie. I'm sure you'll like him."

The End

Within minutes you're playing the Doom 800. It's better than it ever was—the colors are really vivid. And the machine doesn't accept money—you can play as much as you like for free!

"Haven't lost the old touch," you say proudly, blowing on your fingertips. Although it feels like mere minutes, when you check your watch you find out you've been playing for more than an hour.

It might be a good idea to head home. Your parents will wonder where you are. And Mr. Sticks will probably return any second now. No telling what he might do if he found you messing around with his video games.

You give the Doom 800 a loving tap good-bye.

Then the lights go out.

Turn to page 46.

There is silence for a few minutes. "We already have a player for Worm Wars. Mr. Eddie Wrigley. You have been selected as the player for Rat Race. No exceptions."

Small beads of sweat are starting to form on your forehead. Rat Race is Joey's game. He loves it, and he's always asking you to play. But you've never bothered to—you're always too busy with Worm Wars. Desperately you try to remember how the game is played. More importantly, how are players killed?

Turn to page 34.

"What's so hard about pinball?" asks a kid waiting to play Monster Squasher at the machine next to you. "All you do is hit that little ball around. It's just luck if you get a good score."

"Luck?" says Joey, rolling his eyes. "Skill is more like it. Have you ever seen a person play like this?" He points to you.

You give a quick smile but stay focused on the game. Even without your lucky cap, you're doing great! After playing for more than ten minutes with your first ball, you're on to your second. But already your score is higher than it has ever been.

Before you know it, an hour has gone by. At first kids were gathering around, encouraging you. But now they have started to leave—it's getting close to dinnertime.

"Okay, okay. Enough already," Joey says impatiently. He pulls your arm. "You're gonna break the machine if you don't stop soon."

"Back off!" you say, sounding angrier than you mean to. Without taking your eyes off the machine, you say, "My best score can get even better. How can I quit now?"

Turn to page 22.

"Don't go doing something stupid," says Joey. "You're a great player. Forget the hat and stay here with us. You could use the practice before the tournament."

If you decide to go to Mr. Sticks's house, turn to page 37.

If you decide to stay and brush up on your skills, turn to page 58.

Despite what he says, you continue to struggle in the slippery puddle. You can't figure out why you can't get up. Then, to your horror, you realize that the puddle isn't oily—it's filled with fat purple earthworms. They feel like Jell-O. And they stink like rotting meat. The worms squish and squirm under your cold, frightened body.

With every squish you hear a soft moan. "We'll never let you go. We'll never let you go. We'll never let you go."

They mean it.

The End